W9-DGB-519

This book belongs to:

_____

jp

To Zoe, Jessie & Maddie – May your lives
be filled with magical creativity. – M.S.

To my children, Cole and Annabel, who bring
so much magic into my life. – S.S.

Scarlet's Magic Paintbrush
Copyright © 2018 by Melissa Stoller
Artwork Copyright © 2018 by Sandie Sonke
Edited and Art Directed by Mira Reisberg www.childrensbookacademy.com

Summary: Scarlet paints perfect pictures with her magic paintbrush until the day the brush is lost, and she fears she'll never be
able to paint again. When the brush is found, will Scarlet's own magical creativity emerge?

Clear Fork Publishing
P.O. Box 870 102 S. Swenson Stamford, Texas 79553 (325)773-5550 www.clearforkpublishing.com

Printed and Bound in the United States of America.

ISBN - 978-1-946101-67-9
LCN - 2018947254

Scarlet's Magic Paintbrush

Written by
Melissa Stoller

Illustrated by
Sandie Sonke

SPORK

One day, Scarlet found a magic paintbrush and everything changed. She whispered what she wanted, and perfect fairies, unicorns, and princesses magically filled her canvases.

Everything was perfect.
Until . . .

Scarlet lost her magic paintbrush.

She peeked under
her bed.

She gazed into her dollhouse.

She looked in her treehouse.
Her paintbrush was gone.

"Don't worry, you'll paint again," said Mom.
"Of course you will," said Dad.

"Not without my brush," said Scarlet.
"I'll never be able to paint like before."

Mom bought Scarlet a new paintbrush.
Scarlet waited, then tried.
"I like the sand dunes in your painting," said Mom.
Scarlet frowned.
"Those are pancakes."

Scarlet's sister offered a different paintbrush.
"Cute dinosaur," she said.

Scarlet cringed.
"Uh, that's our bunny, Bugsy."

Dad presented her with another new paintbrush that night.

"I could eat those fluffy marshmallows and chocolate chips for dessert," he said.

"Grrr, those are the clouds and stars outside my window."
Scarlet stomped to her room.
Would she ever be able to paint like before?

Scarlet tried painting with her left hand but the brush kept slipping.

Still, she liked the strong lines leaping across the canvas.

Scarlet made a paintbrush using a stick and cotton balls.

That didn't work either.

Yet when she squinted,
bold shapes took flight.

Scarlet even tried finger painting. It was messy, but the swirls and whirls made her smile . . . for a little while.

Scarlet sighed. Would she ever be able to paint like before?

Scarlet searched for her brush some more.

She peered into the bird's cage.

She glanced under the dog's bed.

She hunted through her toy box. Until finally . . .

There it was!
Stuck in her pillowcase!

Then a strange thing happened.

She asked the magic brush to paint a flying dragon,
and it did . . .

but Scarlet had wanted a purple dragon, not green.

She told the brush to paint a prince's birthday party, and it did . . .

but Scarlet had expected more balloons.

She commanded the
brush to paint a castle
in the sky, and it did . . .

but Scarlet had
pictured a moat.

The paintings were perfect.
But none looked the way
Scarlet wanted.

She tried to add details.
The brush wouldn't let her.
"I want to paint my way," she
told the brush.
But nothing changed. Until . . .

grrr

Scarlet picked up the magic brush and placed it
in her desk drawer.

She dipped a new brush
into paint and held it
over a canvas.

Scarlet

She took a deep breath
and smiled, her mind
full of images.

Scarlet painted fairies, unicorns, and princesses.
Flying dragons, birthday parties, castles, and more.

She used strong lines, bold shapes,
swirls, and whirls.
They weren't perfect, but they were hers.

With her own magic,
she painted what she saw
in her heart . . .

Scarlet's Masterpiece.

Melissa Stoller loves creating stories. She once wished for a magic pen, but now she knows better. Melissa lives in New York City with her husband, three daughters, and one puppy. Her chapter book series, *The Enchanted Snow Globe Collection*, takes readers on time-travel adventures. *Scarlet's Magic Paintbrush* is her debut picture book.

www.MelissaStoller.com

Sandie Sonke is a Southern California native and a Cal State University Fullerton grad with a degree in studio art. She finds joy simply sketching in her sketchbook or drawing tablet. Wearer of many hats, Sandie is a freelance illustrator, wife, and mom to two sweet and silly kids who inspire her daily. She loves to create whimsical and colorful illustrations. Her hope is to bring a little happiness to those who view her work.

www.sandiesonkeillustration.com

Find more beautiful children's books at http://bit.ly/CFP_Spork

CPSIA information can be obtained
at www.ICGtesting.com
Printed in the USA
LVHW072030261118
598288LV00029B/634/P